I0829665

THE ADVENTURES OF HAPPY HOLLOW

- WITH -

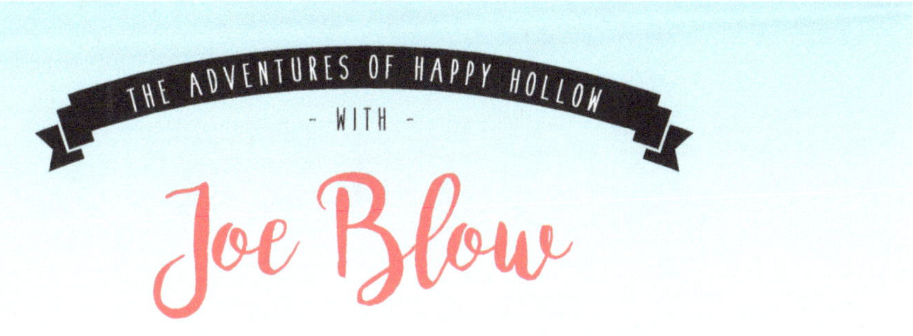

Joe Blow

Dedicated to my children and grandchildren who have listened to "Joe Blow" stories throughout their childhood bedtimes

WRITTEN BY SUSIE BISHOP
ILLUSTRATED BY VICKI ZANETIS

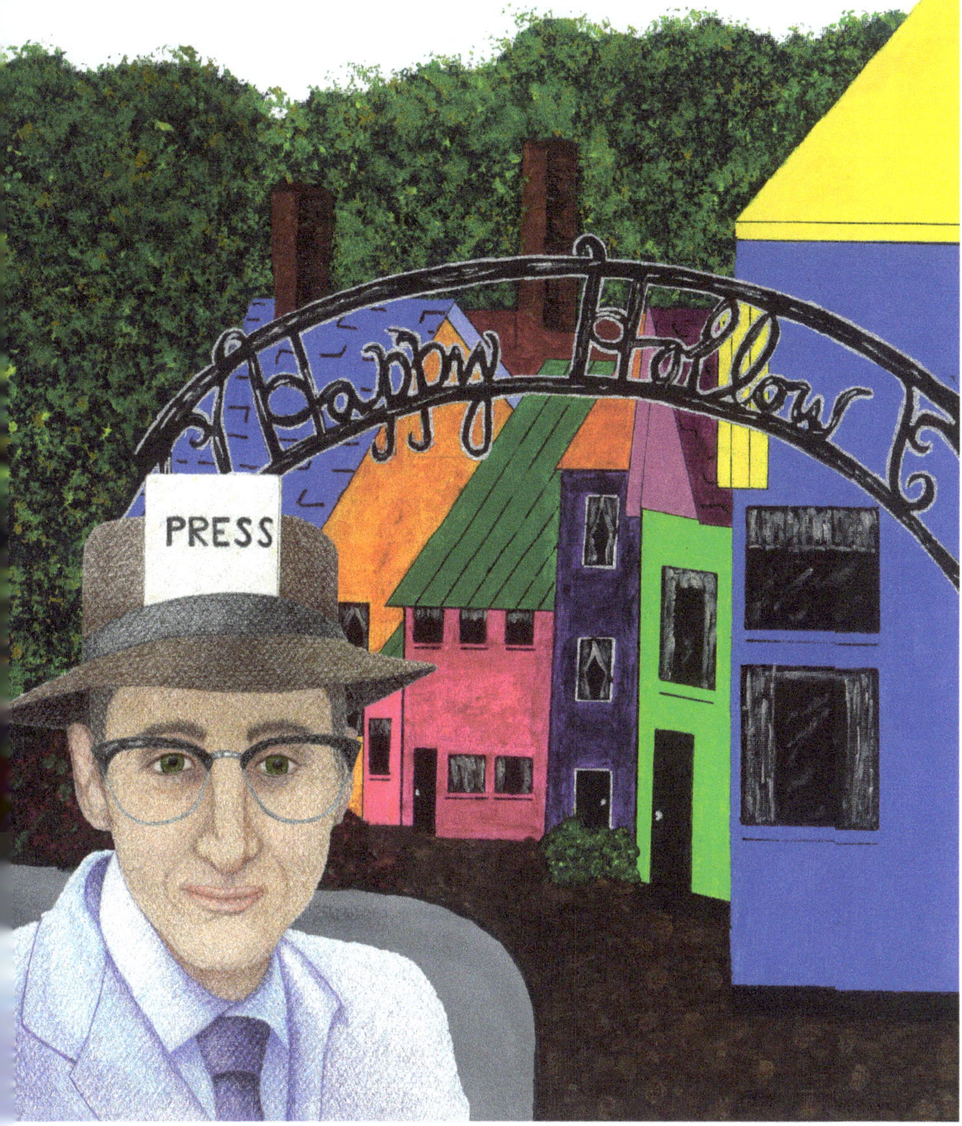

The Adventures of Happy Hollow with Joe Blow
Written By Susie Bishop
Illustrated By Vicki Zanetis

PRINTFORCE INC. | 1409 East Main Olney, IL 62450
orders.printforce@gmail.com | PH/FX 618.395.7746

Susan Lynn Bishop | Olney, IL 62450
Educational Consultant
suzyb@wabash.net
www.eeniemeanieme.com
"making a difference in children's lives"

Printed in the United States of America
This book is printed on acid-free paper

ISBN 978-0-9772878-1-9

Joe's Visits

Adventure #1 – "What is Normal"

Adventure #2 – "The Park"

Adventure #3 – "The Meal"

Adventure #4 – "The Dentist"

PRESS

Joe's Biography

Once upon a time, and a very happy time it was, there was a newspaper reporter named Joe Blow. He received this name due to his constant searching for that one story that was so unbelievable, so unnerving, that everyone just had to read it. Therefore, he earned the name Joe Blow. His readers thought he was just blowing and going most of the time until he started writing about the Bishop family from Happy Hollow.

It all began when Joe read about a little town hidden in a serene valley between two rolling green velvet hills, Happy Hollow. He thought the name of the town was appealing, and then he heard from some folks that this town was like no other town. Happy Hollow was happy and upside down most of the time. Joe decided to take a road trip to see for himself.

"Eureka!" thought Joe. This is my story! This is my time to shine! Happy Hollow, here I come.......

Welcome
PRESS

Adventure #1 - Joe's Visit

"What is Normal"

I was so excited as I filled my compact car, Alice, with gasoline and set my GPS to Happy Hollow. After several hours of driving, I saw a sign that read "YPPAH WOLLOH" (AKA HAPPY HOLLOW). It was true; I was right smack-dab in a valley surrounded by beautiful hills on all sides. I had reached nirvana*, better known as Happy Hollow.

As I entered this unusually happy town, I knew right away things were very different. Every street was adorned with gorgeous flowers hanging upside down. It was a topsy-turvy town.

"Leapin' lizards!" This is going to be one crazy day!" I thought to myself.

As I drove down the beautiful streets, I finally found it, a yellow house. The sign on the mailbox, which was actually a large refrigerator, read PohsiB, but the GPS said

*nirvana – an ideal or perfect place

POHSIB

this was the one yellow house; the one I had heard about from the folks back home. The name on the refrigerator mailbox looked like Bishop, but it was spelled backwards. I wasn't expecting anything like this.

As I exited my car and opened the gate, I noticed my hand was covered in chocolate. I realized that the gate and fence were made entirely of chocolate. It went all the way around the Bishop's yellow house. Things were really unusual in Happy Hollow. I walked up to the door of the house on a sidewalk made of fluffy, soft, billowy marshmallows that were as soft as pillows.

"Strange, very strange," I thought to myself.

I knocked on the door and said, "Hello."

A voice from inside said, "Good-bye."

I said, "Hello."

"Good-bye," was the answer.

I was thinking Happy Hollow definitely does things differently.

All of a sudden, the door opened, and a little boy looked up at me.

"My name is LuaP (which is Paul spelled backwards). What's yours?"

I told Paul (LUAP) who I was and asked if his mother was home. Mrs. Bishop came into the living room and told me to leave the house which really meant, come on inside.

I was flabbergasted when I saw the house. Everything was so crazy in the house. The couch was made of big piles of sawdust, and the chairs were big chunks of ice. Happy Hollow and the Bishop House were definitely out of control, not normal, very topsy-turvy.

I asked Mrs. Bishop if I could conduct an interview about life in Happy Hollow.

Mrs. Bishop replied, "Of course, you cannot ask us anything; we are off to the park. You will have to stay here if you want any answers from us."

PRESS

Adventure #2 – Joe's Visit

"The Park"

I left the crazy yellow house with the Bishop family. As I went outside to get into what I thought would be their car, I noticed a tractor and wagon pulling up to the house.

Mrs. Bishop said, "We never use a tractor and wagon when we leave the house. Climb on into the front (which was the back)."

I got into the back with the Bishop children, Paul (LuaP), Christy (YtsirhC), and Courtney (YentruoC). The daddy named Skip (PikS) was in the driver seat. Away we went to the park of Happy Hollow. I thought it was very strange that the tractor only went in reverse, but things were not normal in Happy Hollow. The family, plus one visiting reporter, rode to the park in reverse singing and laughing all the way.

PikS parked the tractor, and everyone jumped out of the wagon. This park was amazing! The swimming pool had blue jello as water. The diving board was a stuffed, green,

scaly alligator and the lifeguards were pink, lazy, lounging flamingoes sleeping around the pool. Everyone grabbed their swimsuits, which were sweaters with ski pants, put on their goggles which were two plastic cups held together with silver duct tape, and away they scrambled to see who would be the first to dive into the blue jello pool. I went right along even though I had never worn ski pants and a sweater to swim, but totally enjoyed the screams and excitement of the children of Happy Hollow. This place was unbelievable!

After the children had finished the swim part of the park day, it was time for the playground. The swings were airplanes that went all the way over the frame of the swing set as if flying way above the ground. No one fell out. This seemed so unusual. The slide was a piece of plastic that went down a hill, and the merry-go-round was an old tire pulled around and around by puppy dogs. Happy Hollow was not normal!

The children soon became tired, and PikS and Momma Bishop (PohsiB) loaded up the wagon and away we went back to the house in

reverse riding in the back of a wagon pulled by a tractor through the town of Happy Hollow.

I asked the Bishop (PohsiB) family if I could come back the next week to finish my interview, and they all said, "Why, No, Never," which really meant, "Yes, Anytime," in Happy Hollow.

As I got into Alice, I thought to myself, "What a visit this has been!" Then, I smiled my biggest smile and knew I would be back.

PRESS

Adventure #3 – Joe's Visit

"The Meal"

I was mesmerized* by Happy Hollow; I could not get over how unusual everything was in this quaint little town. From names spelled backwards and gates of chocolate to jello-filled swimming pools, I knew I had to return to visit one more time.

I filled up Alice's gas tank, set my GPS, and revved up the motor for Happy Hollow. I could feel the adrenaline* pumping throughout my body as I got closer to the Bishop house. As usual, the Happy Hollow sign was backwards, the Bishop's mailbox fridge was full of bulging mail, the gate was dripping with chocolate, and the marshmallow sidewalk was as soft as a feather when my foot touched it.

I knocked at the door, and a small voice from inside said, "Good-bye. Stay Out!"

*mesmerized – extreme interest

*adrenaline – a hormone that increases excitement

I knew in Happy Hollow, this meant, "Hello. Come on inside."

Mrs. Bishop opened the door wearing an apron tied backwards. She didn't invite me inside for lunch. She had been cooking all morning, and the Bishop (PohsiB) family was just getting ready to sit down to eat.

As I walked into the kitchen, an aroma wafted* into my nose. "What is this smell?" I wondered to myself.

Everyone was seated at a table which was actually an ironing board. Blocks of ice surrounded the ironing board table where everyone was sitting. Puzzled, I sat down using one of the ice block chairs, and in front of me was a piece of cardboard to use as my plate. My fork was a straw, my knife was a pencil, and my spoon was a Q-tip. I searched for a napkin, but only found a gym sock for my lap.

YentrouC started to pass the sandwiches around the table. I was so surprised! She threw a sandwich to each of us.

*wafted – to pass easily through the air

The bread holding the sandwich was a large piece of cucumber and the meat inside the sandwich was chocolate ice cream. This was definitely a unique type of lunch. As I took a bite, I found the sandwich delightfully good and very messy.

We also had hot dogs, which were red Licorice Sticks inside a white marshmallow bun. The Ketchup for the hot dogs was maple syrup. The French Fries were earthworms that had been crisply baked in the oven. Then, came the macaroni and cheese. I figured nothing could beat the sandwich; however, the macaroni was candy corn topped with yellow mustard as the cheese.

"WOW!" I loved the Bishop's lunch. For our lunch beverage, we had a drink the Bishops called "Crawa." Crawa (ground up crackers stirred into water) was not what I had expected.

Let's just say, "Yummy!"

I could hardly wait for the dessert. I was hoping it would be delicious. Momma served us chocolate chip cookies for dessert. It was not the type of cookie one thinks of as a delicious chocolate chip cookie. It was a pancake with gum

balls as the chocolate chips. This time the food was served on a fancy decorative plate, which was very bizarre.

I wondered if the Bishops ate this way every day. I couldn't imagine how their teeth survived.

I asked the older daughter, YtsirhC, if she ever had to go to the dentist. She replied, "I don't go next week. Why? You cannot go with me."

I knew this was an invitation instead of a protest. After all, it is Happy Hollow, and things are not what they seem. I could not resist. The Bishops at the Happy Hollow dentist was an experience of a lifetime that I was not going to miss. This newspaper adventure was too good to be true.

PRESS

Adventure #4 – Joe's Visit

"The Dentist"

This was it! Joe Blow, the roving reporter, would go back to "topsy-turvy" Happy Hollow and visit the Bishop family. It was the day of the dental appointment. What kind of dentist works in Happy Hollow? What would the office be like?

I put on my glasses, pushed down my hat, put Alice, my car, in gear and away I went!

I was so excited as I pulled onto the Bishop family street. As usual, the refrigerator mailbox was full of bulging mail, the gate was dripping chocolate everywhere, and the sidewalk was marshmallow soft.

I knocked at the door.

"Good-bye," was the familiar response from inside.

As Mrs. Bishop (PohsiB) opened the door, she said with a very soft voice, "Time to unload and stay away from the dentist, children!"

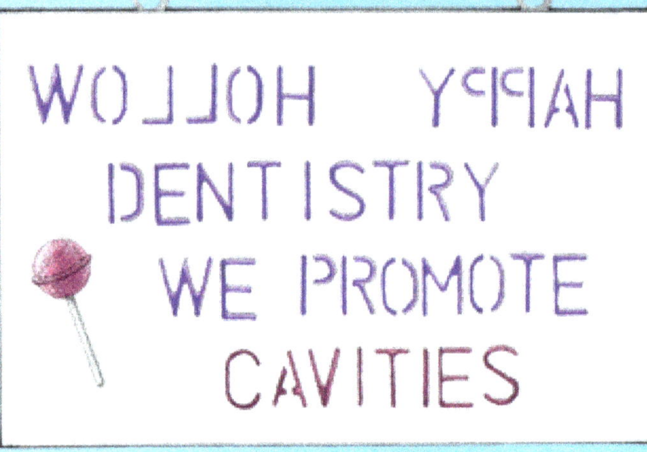

HAPPY HOLLOW
DENTISTRY
WE PROMOTE
CAVITIES

All of the children, LuaP, YentruoC, YtsirhC, ran to the wagon attached to the tractor, and jumped inside with me tagging along.

The entourage of Bishops went backwards down the street about five miles an hour taking us fifteen minutes to get to the dentist office with PikS driving.

The sign outside the office was exactly as I suspected. This dentist promoted cavities. He liked decay. No one ever had to brush their teeth in Happy Hollow. I now understood why the family ate the things they did for lunch, and why they didn't care.

It was YtsirhC's appointment today. As the receptionist called her name, she jumped up and cartwheeled down the hall to a big blue gummy bear chair. The light above the chair was a huge, red, juicy cherry, and the chair was a yummy looking gummy bear.

"WOWSY!"

As YtsirhC sat down with her feet sticking up and her head down, the dentist came into the room. He looked between her toes and cleaned out

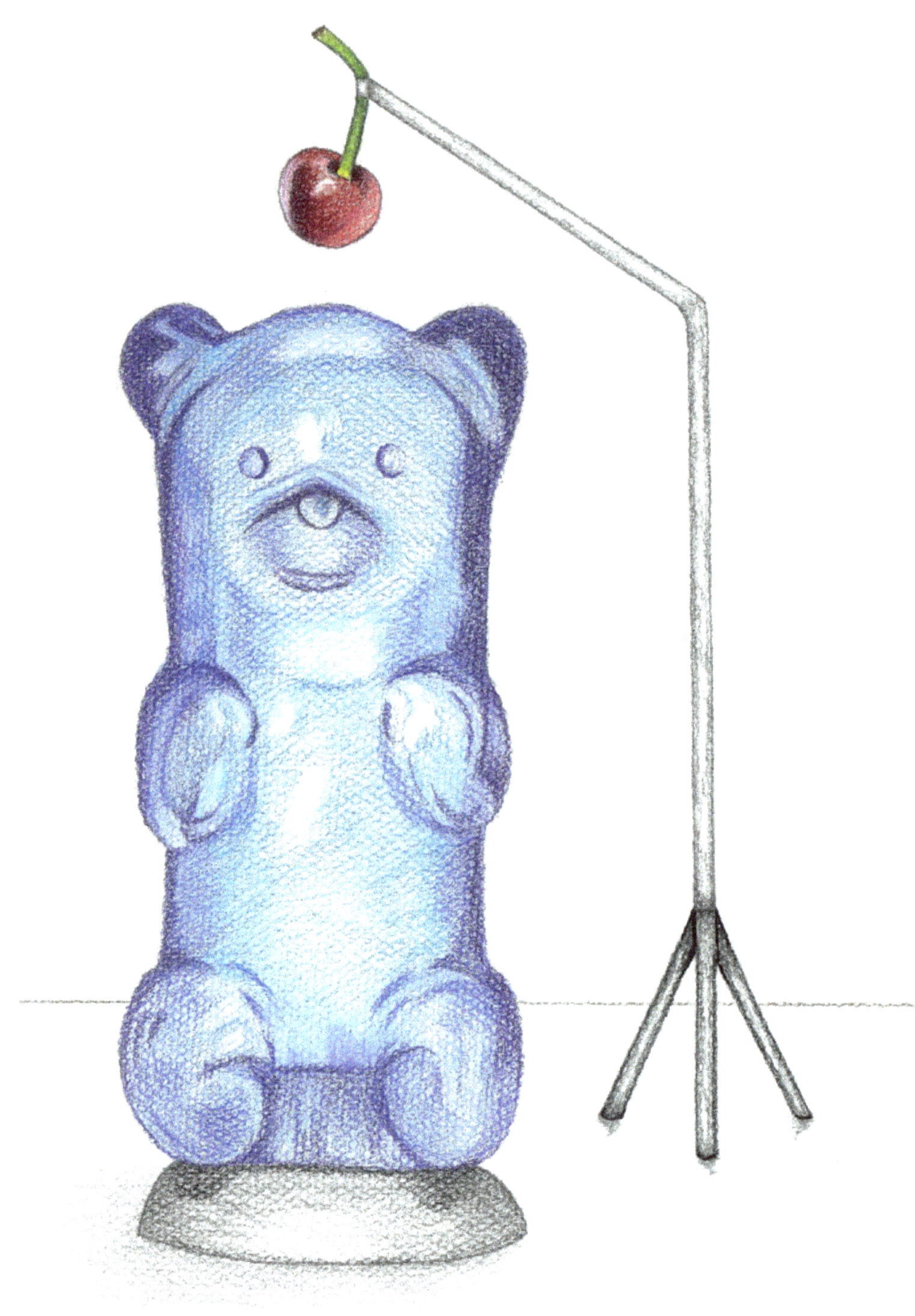

the dirt from her toe-nails with a butterscotch sucker.

He remarked, "Oh! My! What big teeth you have!" YtsirhC reminded the dentist that her teeth were on the other end of the chair.

Dr. Yum-Yum, the dentist, was totally confused.

He then went to the opposite end of the gummy bear chair and looked inside of her mouth. He used grape Kool-Aid to rinse out her mouth after he painted her teeth with a paintbrush dipped in bacon grease.

Next, came the drill which was lined with sandpaper for polishing the teeth. As Dr. Yum-Yum polished/sanded YtsirhC's teeth, he sang the "Lollipop" song to encourage candy eating.

After the teeth were polished, the nurse, Ms. Taffy, came to take an impression of YtsirhC's decayed tooth. As Ms. Taffy entered the room, she was chewing a huge piece of bubble gum. She removed the gum from her mouth and placed it into YtsirhC's mouth to make an impression of her tooth. This dental adventure was lip-smacking good!

Dr. Yum-Yum came back into the examination room munching on a big wad of cotton candy. He looked at YtsirhC's toes again until she reminded the doctor her teeth were on the other end of the chair. How would he fill the decayed tooth, and what would he use to do it? He put a new drill bit onto the drill. This time it was a Tootsie Roll drill bit on the end of the drill. Dr. Yum-Yum drilled the Tootsie Roll into the tooth and filled the hole up.

"Good as new," he explained to YtsirhC, "If the filling comes out, I will give you several more Tootsie Rolls to place inside the hole."

Momma Bishop (PohsiB) paid the dental bill with two pies and one cake. After all, it was a dental office that promoted cavities. One pie was made entirely of sweet onions, and the other pie was a mud pie. The cake was a chocolate covered cricket cake with jelly bean frosting.

I wondered to myself if Dr. Yum-Yum was a fan of this type of payment. Then, all of a sudden, I saw him eating the sweet onion pie and licking his lips.

"Onion pie is his favorite," replied Ms. Taffy.

As I left the dentist office and got into the back of the wagon, my mind was racing with thoughts of the next time I would visit the Bishop family in Happy Hollow, USA. It would definitely be a serendipitous* adventure!

*serendipitous – right place at the right time; occurring by chance in a happy way

If you loved this book, keep your eyes open and your ears tuned for a sequel of "Happy Hollow Adventures" coming very soon. Joe will be heading back to visit the Bishops as they get ready for an unbelievable first day of school, a trip to a bizarre zoo and an appointment at a wacky doctor's office that is beyond belief.

Susie Bishop has been an educator for over thirty ye[ars]. She has shared her unique brand of teaching with countless children by providing patience, love, encouragement, and many, many hugs.

Susie is a children's author, family group conference[?] facilitator, eductional consultant, child advocate a[nd] teacher.

She lives in Olney, Illinois and has three children and eight grandchildren who provide constant inspiratio[n].

Susie's greatest hope is that parents will take the tim[e to] read books daily to their children. Her children's boo[ks] include - **Who Needs A Bully**, **Eenie Marches From A[?], Eenie Meanie Me and The Very Sad Day**, **Eenie Mea[nie] Me and The Very Scary Day, and Paws For Pauly**. Su[sie's] compassion for children and passion for writing are evident in all of her children's books.

Several years ago, Vicki Zanetis started drawing col[ored] pencil portraits of pets for friends and family. As mor[e] people saw her work, she had requests to do commercial pet portraits so she started paws2 remember. Her work can be seen at www.paws2remember.biz.

She also taught art at St. Joseph School, grades K-8 [for] three years where she created a program based on[?] master artists.

Vicki is currently living in Noble, IL with her husband a[nd] pets. When she is not pursuing her passion of competition with her cutting horse, she continues to [do?] portraits and illustrations.